If I Could Be My Grandmother

by Steven Kroll

illustrated by Lady McCrady

Pantheon Books

For Lincoln and Odile
and their grandmother

Text Copyright © 1977 by Steven Kroll.
Illustrations Copyright © 1977 by Lady McCrady.
All rights reserved under International and Pan-American Copyright Conventions.
Published in the United States by Pantheon Books, a division of Random House, Inc.,
and simultaneously in Canada by Random House of Canada Limited, Toronto.

Library of Congress Cataloging in Publication Data

Kroll, Steven. If I could be my grandmother.

Summary: A young girl describes all that she would do if she were her grandmother.
[1. Grandmothers—Fiction] I. McCrady, Lady. II. Title. PZ7.K9225If
[E] 77-4321 ISBN 0-394-83554-9 ISBN 0-394-93554-3 lib. bdg.
Manufactured in the United States of America. 0 1 2 3 4 5 6 7 8 9

If I could
be my
grandmother

I'd wear long robes and big hats

and keep my house very neat

and have lots of pictures of my family.

I'd have plants
on my windowsill
and water them a lot.

I'd keep candy in a dish on the table

and have my friends in for lunch.

I'd show them my granddaughter's new paintings

and then I'd hang the paintings in the kitchen.

I'd take an umbrella to the beach

and watch everyone go swimming.

I'd solve all the family problems without trying

and understand when Mother doesn't

and go to everyone's graduation

and come to visit when someone was sick.

I'd ask my granddaughter to visit every weekend

and we'd bake cookies

and play any games
she wanted

and go to the museum

and talk a lot

and read two stories before she went to sleep

and love each other very much.

And in the morning we'd get up together

and have cornflakes for breakfast.

Some day
I'll be
a grandmother
too.